GW00870304

The Magician's Plot

By Sandra Hanna

Grosvenor House
Publishing Limited

This book is published by
Grosvenor House Publishing Ltd
Link House
140 The Broadway, Tolworth, Surrey, KT6 7HT.
www.grosvenorhousepublishing.co.uk

This book is a work of fiction. Any resemblance to
people or events, past or present, is purely coincidental.

A CIP record for this book
is available from the British Library

ISBN 978-1-80381-338-7

Dedication

For our precious girls:

Alex and Lucy   Philippa and Ozma

Jacqui and Grace

And Lily

And for mothers and daughters everywhere

Inspired by and in memory of Connie, Audrey and Jack

"We will all be together again one day"

Part 1

Missing by Magic

Many, many years ago -
A hundred or more, as far as I know,
A young girl sat on a garden swing,
As her father pushed her she'd laugh and she'd sing,

"Swing me high, swing me low,
Swing me up and away,
Swing me over the moon
To the Milky Way!"

Then after she'd swung to her heart's content,
She scooped up her kitten and inside they went.
Her mother had made a surprise for tea,
She rushed inside wondering what it could be.

3

On the table she saw her favourite honey,
It dripped from the jar, all golden and runny,
Next to it a loaf of freshly baked bread
And butter as yellow as a buttercup's head!

After tea she scampered upstairs,
As she did every night before saying her prayers,
And listening to stories of fairies and sprites,
Of giants, princesses and dragon-slaying knights.

The girl pulled the covers right up to her chin,
As the storyteller settled down to begin,
But just as the knight was conquering his foes,
Sleep won the battle, her eyes started to close.

When her mother was sure that she slept,
She kissed her child gently and downstairs she crept.
The smoky-grey kitten snuggled next to the girl
And soon joined his friend in their dreamtime world.

Downstairs the young man hugged his pretty young wife,
She smiled at him, they were happy with life!

Next morning, the family sat happily round
Their table, for breakfast,
Unaware that the sound of their laughter and fun
Had reached the ears of an evil one.

He was a magician, and as you will see,
Dark magic was his vile currency!
When the sound of joy assaulted his ears,
He would quickly plot to turn laughter to tears!

That same morning, in different guise,
He waited for the family to say their goodbyes.
He watched from a distance, until he saw
The smiling young girl, appear at the door.

Her mother had sent her out to play,
While she washed the dishes and put them away.

The girl's father followed close behind,
He kissed his daughter and warned,

"Now, mind you stay this side of the gate!"
Then he rushed down the path, unaware of their fate.

The day was warm, the sky clear blue,
Spring flowers sparkled in the morning dew.
A robin that had made the garden his home
Perched on the head of a garden gnome.

The young girl decided to pick daffodils
To bring sunshine to their windowsills.
As she gathered the flowers she sang to herself,
A song for her friend, the daffodil elf,

8

"Oh, little elf, come out to play,
Out with me on this springtime day,
Your home is golden, like the sun,
Please come out here and have some fun!"

She carefully inspected each trumpet, in case
She could catch a glimpse of her elf friend's face!

But just as she picked the final flower,
Around about the ninth hour,
A beautiful butterfly circled her head,
Its huge wings patterned in purple and red.

It alighted silently on the gatepost,
As the girl drew close, she could hear the most
Beautiful music, that seemed to come
From the butterfly's wings, like a heavenly hum!

She moved even closer and reached out her hand,
Hoping to tempt the creature to land,
Just when she thought it was going to stay,
It fluttered its wings and flew further away.

The mystical music streamed into her mind,
Very soon she had left the garden behind.
As farther away from her home she strayed,
She forgot the warning her father gave.

Her walk turned quickly into a dance,
As the butterfly lured her away, in a trance,
She followed those wings of purple and red,
Deeper into the woods she was led.

Her father was starting work at the farm
When a familiar robin raised the alarm,
It was singing an eerie and urgent song,

Calling him,

    Warning him,

        Something was WRONG!

At that moment the girl's father knew
His child was in danger.
What could he do?

14

The robin flew ahead of him into the wood,
He knew he must follow as fast as he could!
He raced on, his eyes fixed firmly ahead,
Along the overgrown path he sped.

The trees and flowers around him blurred
As he desperately followed the red-breasted bird.
The robin stopped suddenly and then disappeared,
What the young man saw was worse than he feared!

There in front of him was his child,
She was standing and staring, completely beguiled,
As the scene unfolding in front of their eyes
Saw the creature abandon his cunning disguise.

From the beautiful wings of purple and red
There emerged scrawny arms, cloaked in black, and,
Instead of the velvety body was the crooked form
Of the evil magician, now completely transformed!

The father rushed to his daughter's side,
The wizard raised bony hands and cried,

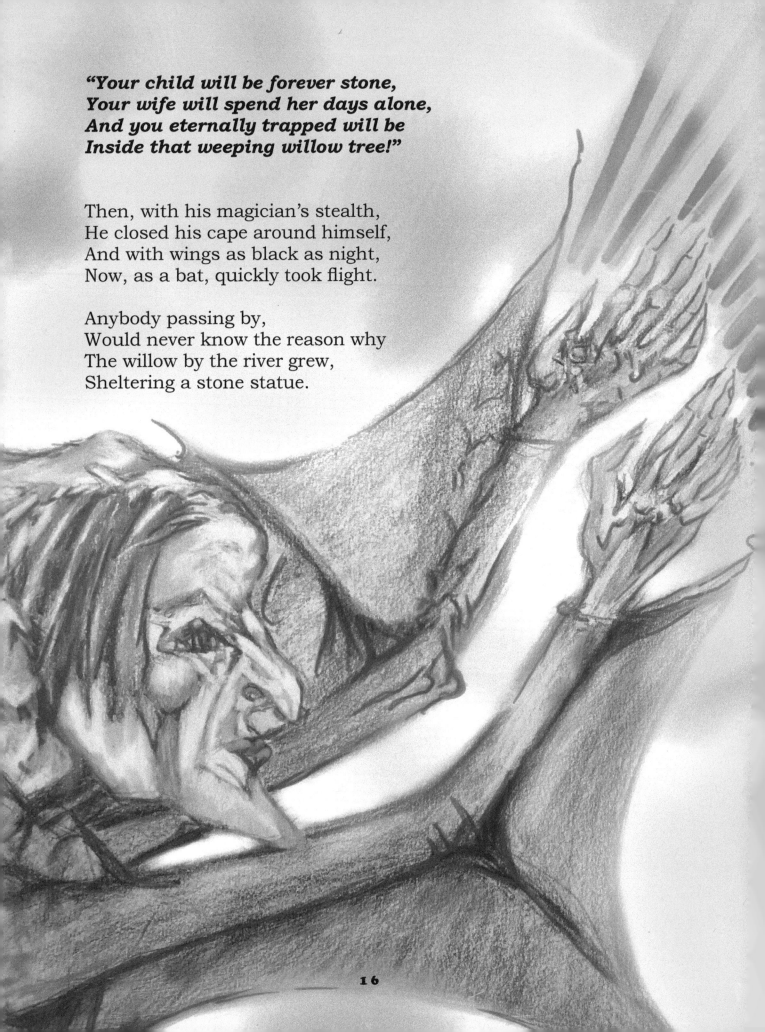

"Your child will be forever stone,
Your wife will spend her days alone,
And you eternally trapped will be
Inside that weeping willow tree!"

Then, with his magician's stealth,
He closed his cape around himself,
And with wings as black as night,
Now, as a bat, quickly took flight.

Anybody passing by,
Would never know the reason why
The willow by the river grew,
Sheltering a stone statue.

At the cottage, meanwhile, the young woman cried
For her young daughter to come inside,
To help her make the daily bread,
That kept the family nicely fed.

But, no footsteps on the path were heard,
No chattering, not a single word,
Not even the sound of a chirruping bird!

The young woman wiped her hands and then
Went to the door to call again,
But what she saw caused her dismay,
For instead of seeing her child at play,
She saw the path that could not be seen
When the gate was closed, as it should have been!

Her knees grew weak,
Her blood ran cold,
Her daughter hadn't done as she was told!

Hurriedly, she set off to find her child,
And as she searched her thoughts ran wild.
She decided to go to the place where
Her husband worked, hoping she'd be there.

Breathless and anxious she arrived at the farm,
Hoping her daughter had come to no harm.
But no one had seen and no one had heard
Her husband leave without a word,
Following the tiny bird.

And NO ONE knew that her child was now stone.
In despair, the young woman went home alone.

Sadly, neither returned at the end of the day,
So this continued as the months passed away.
Spring turned to summer and as the earth spun around,
Golden leaves tumbled and covered the ground.

The days grew short,
The nights grew cold,
Still she searched,
As the year grew old.

A woman stood on a carpet of white,
Trees silhouetted against a darkening sky.

The river that daily ran noisily past,
Was silent and still, like frosted glass.

As she looked at the surface the woman could see,
Her distorted reflection, so sad was she,
For instead of a smile that could light up the skies,
Her face was drawn; there was pain in her eyes.

Again the swirling flakes came down,
Once more she'd have to turn around,
Retrace her steps, find her way home,
But her prints had been covered by drifting snow,
And she didn't know which way to go.

Still she trudged, until at last,
With snowflakes falling thick and fast,
She huddled down beneath a tree
And, exhausted, drifted into sleep.

As she slept, she dreamed a dream,
She saw them together beside a stream.
She saw her husband pushing a swing,
And she heard the sweet voice of her daughter sing,

"Swing me high, swing me low,
Swing me up and away,
We will all be together again one day!"

But as she moved closer, they faded from sight,
Then she felt gentle hands holding her tight.
She was lifted and cradled, enveloped in love
And nestled in feathers, soft as those of a dove.

25

When the woman awoke she was in her own bed,
With the smoky- grey cat curled up by her head.
She didn't know how she came to be there,
Or why the feeling of despair had faded,
Like her greying hair.

But she felt a peace she had never known,
She knew she would never be alone,
For although her family had been taken away
By an evildoer on that fateful day,
She knew GOOD would triumph and LOVE would restore
Her husband and daughter to her once more!

Part 2

The Stone Child

An old woman sat in her old rocking chair,
Firelight glowed on her face and her hair,
She rocked and she dreamed of times gone by,
While her old grey cat swatted a fly,
That had landed on the tip of his nose
And woken him up from his 'Old Cat' dose.

As the old woman stared at the flickering fire,
She watched as the flames grew higher and higher,

Next a strange thing happened, to her surprise,
She stopped rocking, leaned forward and screwed up her eyes.

She screwed up her eyes in order to peer
At the shifting shapes that NOW became CLEAR!

In the parting flames was a pretty young child,
For an instant their eyes met, the old woman smiled.
Then the young girl pleaded, a tear in her eye,
The old woman thought she heard a faint cry,

"Help me, help me please,
I'm trapped near the river,
Next to old willow trees!"

Then the girl was gone and in her place,
Lurked an evil smile on an evil face. Next–

A FLASH!

A BANG!

And a cloud of smoke billowed from the grate,
Made Old Cat choke!

Old Woman froze in her old rocking chair,
Moonlight streamed through the window on silvery hair.
She sat and she wondered what this could mean,
Pondering on the things that she'd seen,

In her mind she could still hear the young girl cry,
She decided that night, that tomorrow she'd try
To find the girl and set her free,
But now it was time for a strong cup of tea!

At last, she picked up her nightlight,
Climbed the stairs up to bed,
With the face of the wee one stuck in her head.

Old Cat washed his paws, settled down in the gloom,
Soon the snores of the pair rattled the room!

In just a few hours the sun's rays broke through
And danced on the eyes of the sleeping two.
Up they both got and descended the stairs,
Their old boned creaked like those 'apples and pears'!

After breaking their fast, with porridge and fish,
Old Woman stood, as if making a wish,
As Old Cat gave his bowl one last lick,
Old Woman picked up her bag and her stick.

Then she stepped outside, followed by Old Cat,
She locked the door, put the key in her hat,
She NEVER left it under the mat!

The day was good, with a clear blue sky –
Except for cumulous clouds floating by.
As Old Woman gazed at the clouds she could see
A child standing beneath a willow tree,
The girl beckoned and called, *"Come follow me!"*

Then the girl was gone and in her place,
Shone a radiant smile on a radiant face.

Although the day was sunny and bright,
There streamed from the sky, a brilliant light!
It didn't light the path to the wood,
Could this possibly lead to where the girl stood?
It lit the path that not many had trod.
Old Woman followed, although it seemed odd.

The path was narrow, the brambles spikey and thick,
Old Woman cleared them away with her stick.
Past trees, through caves, round crumbling towers,
They journeyed on for several hours,
Where nothing was lit by the rays of the sun,
But they didn't need that old 'currant bun',
For the guiding light that lit their way,
Through the deep, dark places, shone brighter than day!

Now Old Woman stopped for a bite to eat,
Shared with Old Cat, what a treat!
Fed fully up and as tired as can be,
She couldn't get up from the stump of the tree.
Old Cat climbed up, settled down on her lap,
And soon they were taking a welcome catnap!

After forty-four minutes and a half had past,
And Old Cat's eyes were still shut fast,
Old Woman woke with a sudden start,
She felt a strange longing deep down in her heart.

They set off once more and soon noticed that,
The creatures that flew were now owl and bat,
For although they'd set off in the morning that day,
Daytime to nighttime had now given way.

Yet the luminous light still directed their feet
To the place where the wood and the river meet.
Lo and behold were the old willow trees,
Old Woman gasped and fell to her knees!

Old Cat meowed and nuzzled her hand,
Encouraging Old Woman to stand.
Although she was thrilled, her heart filled with fear,
For she sensed the presence of evil near,
Her body chilled,
    Her old heart raced,
        Her Old Woman steps now gathered pace!

She hurried towards a strange looking stone,
That stood by the roots of a tree, on its own.
Beneath the dirt and the moss she made out,
A familiar face, there could be no doubt!

Her arms wrapped around the rocky mass,
And sparkling tears, like crystal glass
Dropped on the stone, and where they fell,
Began to break that wicked spell.

Stone melted away, and in its place,
Beamed a JOYFUL smile on a JOYFUL face.
Tears of love had set her daughter free,
As they hugged each other, neither one could see,
A much-loved face in the willow there
Or the evil face with the *evil* glare,
That snarled, then grumbling disappeared,
LOVE triumphed and *evil* was no longer feared.

But they did hear something, a wondrous sound,
And a great rushing wind swept their feet off the ground.
In a swirl of light they were whisked away,
To their cottage home and the light of day.

Waiting to greet them at the door
Was Old Woman's husband, as he'd been years before.
Old Woman embraced him, and realized that,
She was once again young, and so was Old Cat!

She would no longer rock in her old rocking chair,
Firelight glowing on her face and her hair,
She would no longer dream of times gone past,
Her husband and daughter were home at last!

And all the years that were stolen away,
Disappeared at the dawn of a brand new day,
For GOOD *had* triumphed and LOVE *had* restored
Her husband and daughter to her once more.